Landings (2009)
Field Notes (Volume One) (2012) *
Moor Glisk (2012)
Limnology (2012)
Nimrod is lost in Orion and
Osyris in the Doggestarre (2014)
Memorious Earth (2015) *
Beyond the Fell Wall (2015)
The Pale Ladder (Selected Poems
& Texts 2009–2014) (2016)
Towards a Frontier (2017)
The Look Away (2018)
Dark Hollow Dark (2019)
LASTGLACIALMAXIMUM (2020)

* with Autumn Richardson

AND THEN GONE

RICHARD SKELTON

XYLEM BOOKS 2020

Richard Skelton, *And Then Gone*
First published in 2020 by Corbel Stone Press
This edition copyright © Xylem Books 2020

© Richard Skelton 2020

The author's moral rights have been asserted

ISBN: 978-1-9163935-1-6

Xylem Books is an imprint of Corbel Stone Press

eorþe þe on bere eallum hire mihtum
may earth bear on thee with all her might

Læc Boc
LXIII

I

The fear of open spaces is unlike the fear of cities. Threat of distance over proximity. Restless, living movement of leaves and branches against the dull inertia of buildings, of architecture. But fear is fear, nonetheless.

*

Scene. Road, fields, sky. North country, just south of the wall. Early morning, cold. A car, a woman. Alone.

*

Colours. Grey-green, grey-brown, grey-blue. Her skin taking on each hue like a taint. Grey of the road and of the sky. A pathology.

*

Her idling the car for warmth. A sickness in the stomach, or possibly hunger. She cannot tell. Isn't hunger a sickness, after all?

*

Endless pallor, endless muteness, endless sullen resistance to meaning, endless egress of the world from itself.

*

Moods. Bruised. Eyes looking away. Veiled suffering. Aching.

*

And the road itself lifeless. Not a thick, thrumming vein, close to the heart, but something peripheral, thrombosic. Will it wither to nothing in those far low hills, out to the east?

*

No onslaught of traffic here. No heavenly white noise of engine and friction. No joyous scream of life lived with sharpness.

*

But the road's surface still rutted with use. Not from volume or frequency of traffic, but the inevitable slow degradation of time over time. Attrition, receding into the barren reaches of human forgetting.

*

Life itself, almost from the very outset. Rubbing, wearing, thinning. Becoming translucent.

*

And that attrition. That daily incessant working of friction and gravity, a mere feather stroke. A homologue of something far greater. The tender millennial violence of ice and water. Incomprehensible to human thought in its slow vastness. But the land knowing it, feeling it, remembering it. Unforgiving.

*

All that is, an injuring. Gouge, shatter, scar, fracture.

*

Her looking. Up and down the road's flatness. Outwash plain of her own suffering. This residual violence too vague, too distant, for her to apprehend. A fading, yellowing bruise on already jaundiced skin.

*

And so the world somehow occulted. Wreathed. Opaque to her senses. Her blood sluggish. Her thoughts torpid.

*

Wordless anonymity of the rural. Unreadable trees, hedgerows. Blank-seeming pages of fields. Everything known unto itself but revealing nothing.

*

And vertical and horizontal and vertical and horizontal
and vertical and horizontal and vertical and horizontal.

*

Sameness becoming somehow both sedative and stim-
ulant. Lulling and concussive. The road a line drawn
between the two.

*

Evening. A day somehow passed. The car radio's signal, dried to a thin stream of static, occasionally breaking into sudden torrents of noise. There is comfort in it, nonetheless, and she listens long into the night, curled in the back seat. Voices, humanity, contact. These things are yesterday's vestiges. Tell me again why I am here? Why am I doing this? The image of her mother's tearful face. Go back.

*

Day. The car moving slowly along the road's narrow. She brings it to a stop at a junction. Habitually, she looks left and right, up and down, for traffic, for news. As if on cue the radio spasms into life. There are words but she cannot make them out.

*

Her eyes framed in the rear-view mirror. See her.
Something familial between you. There.

*

The question of which way to go. Is this not the same
road, splitting itself, riddling itself, offering the decep-
tion of choice only to snatch it back, later? Maze of
same-seeming green and grey. Deadened beauty of time
endlessly spooling in these fields and ditches.

*

And green and grey and green and grey and green and
grey. Over and over.

*

Watery call of a curlew in a far-off field. It is remote to her. She cannot resolve that glissandic song into an image of the known. To her it is the shrill, frightened cry of the lost. And yet, deep within the dark fields of her childhood, a bird answers, and its faint voice bubbles up into her consciousness. Fear is another form of knowing.

*

Curlew. Curled beak of the meadow. Circle-bruise of vowels. Diminishing. Dissolving. And then gone.

*

When a bruise fades, what if a mark remains somewhere else? A wound of the skinless skin. How many such bruises should we endure? The fields would tell her, if she would but listen.

*

Each crossroad the same. A multiple of the first. A copy, an instance. Each a variation on the same basal question. She reads the weatherworn sign. Vague backcountry cuneiform, stippled with rust, lichen. Stranded palaeography of the north. And the arrows pointing the wrong way.

*

She plays a child's game of choice with the fingers of one hand. But there is only one way to go. Only onwards. Only forwards. Only.

*

And the straightness of the road. It moves something in her. An eddy in her waters.

*

Morning. Mist. A new blankness. A new anodyne greyness. Forms unforming themselves. Road, fields, sky. Each implicated in the other. The world a narcotic memory of itself.

*

Colours. All that is not mist bleached to blue-grey.

*

She edges onwards. Barely out of first gear. High whine of the engine baffled by the encroaching haze.

*

Distant hills gone. Perspective gone. Earth-flatness a second guess. Perforated theory of light and shade. Proximity everything. Memory reduced to a fine point. Are there even cities any more?

*

Even though it is daylight, and there is no one else on the road, she fumbles on the dashboard for the fog lights.

*

Colours. Incandescent yellow-white of the car's lights leaching away at the greyness.

*

Memory. Drawn to the surface by the lights' heat. A day such as this. The backseat of a car, her parents in the front. Her looking over her father's shoulder at the brightly lit dashboard. His hands on the steering wheel, the left at seven, the right at five. Scent of leather and chocolate. Music on the radio. No. Her father singing. His voice.

*

Her closing her eyes, her foot on the brake. The nearness of it. So close she can touch it. Him. A deep wave
of anguish overcoming her. Palpitations in her throat.
Pinpricks of sweat. Memory, have you hidden here, all
this time, waiting for my return?

*

When her heart settles she opens her eyes again, unpre-
pared for what greets her.

*

*This. Close on her face, dilating eyes. Something reflect-
ing in them.*

*

A stag. Standing before the car. Enveloped in the lights' corona. Seven tines on each of its antlers. The bright tapestry of its eyes an iridescence. The look of it so unreal and so beautiful it steals her breath. She is trembling.

*

The deer momentarily turns its head, perpendicular. Exhales heavily. In the periphery of her vision other shapes, stepping into the light. Lithe doe bodies, emerging from the nothingness of mist and into her consciousness. Their eyes, all of them, glowing, as if their insides burn with the brightness of suns. The stag stands squarely before the car as the others press close. It stamps the ground with a foreleg. She still isn't breathing. This moment, held for an eternity.

*

The stag stamps the ground again, speaks. A deep, guttural sound. Instinctively she reaches for the dashboard to turn off the fog lights.

*

Her watching as the light of the deer's eyes fades. The dying of stars.

*

The low, vibrating hum of the engine against the stillness of the deer. Moments pass like the wheeling of galaxies. She turns the key in the ignition and the car falters into silence.

*

Scene. The blue-greyness of the car and the woman and the deer. This, the entirety of the world. Their forms softened, insubstantial as memory. Eventually the stag turns and walks slowly away, down the road, the others close by. Each of their forms contracting, dissipating, diminishing, until they are mere bruises on grey-white skin. And then gone.

*

Aftermath. A violence to her senses, her mind. Gouge, shatter, scar, fracture.

*

She sits, motionless, hands at the wheel. The left at seven, the right at five. Scent of leather and despair. She turns the radio on. Thin singing stream of static. Its voice.

II

Night. She hasn't moved. The mist finally dispersed by heavy rain. The sound so loud it drowns out the radio. The feel of it on the car's roof. Perforating her body, her consciousness.

*

Dream. A train carriage, empty except for a man with a stranger's face sitting some distance behind her. Her wanting so badly to get off the train, but feeling compelled to stay, unable to leave this man whom she knows and yet does not know. And the journey endless, and through the windows the forms of ruined buildings, engulfed by plants and trees, slipping past her at high speed. Not another person in sight. And her wanting so badly to get off the train.

*

Her waking in the early hours. Silence. She steps out of the car to feel the darkness of the sky, made porous by so many stars. She looks at the constellations and wishes for their names. And as her eyes adjust to the lack of light she sees more and yet more. They seem to multiply at the periphery of her vision. Spawning.

*

Next day. She stares at the sky's milky whiteness and sees only stars. A tremor on her surface, rippling outwards.

*

And in the calm clarity of morning a guttural sound rings out, reverberant, from the far trees beyond the fields. She tries the car but the battery is dead. She tells herself it is the radio. That, unheard during the storm, it had drained the battery's last reserves. That call again. A coldness across her shoulders.

*

Go back? A vestige of resolve held against the uncertainty of these last days. I will walk onwards from here.

*

The road still wet after the night's rain. Sound of water moving slowly in ditches. Something like song.

*

To walk, and to carry my heart in my hands, heavy, glistening.

*

Later. Low on the horizon, a black shape. A whorl of birds, a swirling congregation, far off. As she nears they begin to bark their alarms. On the other side of a field-gate, the subject of their ceremony. A lamb, stillborn. A sudden shiver on her skin.

*

Memory. Rising to her surface like trapped air. A farm cottage in the country and the image of another lamb, born with a congenital deformity. Try as it might, it can never straighten its forelegs and stand. And her, a child, uncomprehending, watching it from her window. Day after day. Trying to stand. A sickness rising inside her. And the mother seemingly senseless, occasionally wandering near to her offspring, and then standing there for a while, looking absently away. Caught between two opposing kinds of instinct. To feed her young, and to abandon the diseased or malformed. And the lamb would struggle, crying feebly, trying to get itself close enough to the teat. But it can never quite reach. As the days pass its strength diminishes, and it spends more and more time motionless. No energy even to cry. And then one day she looks out of her window and the lamb and its mother are gone. And she wishes that she could fill her belly with stones from the river, and sink and sink into the coldness of water.

*

Why shore such things inside ourselves? Why drape them in softness and forget, if they can tear through our consciousness like a knife? Why bury them, if they may come back to life?

*

With effort she blinks away the film of memory from her eyes and focuses on the reality before her. The animal's limbs are twisted as if, in its last moments, it had attempted to embrace itself. To guard itself against the falling in and out of life. And its wool hasn't yet dried.

*

The birds scatter noisily, trailing ribbons of afterbirth. She looks up, her throat tight, a pressing sensation in her temples. Can you feel it?

*

Further up the field there are other lambs and their mothers. They stare blandly. She climbs over the gate and then they too scatter. Reaching up she breaks a spreading branch from an overhanging tree and lays it gently over the diminutive body. It looks like a great arm extended in a gesture of comfort, but it is a futile simulacrum. I can do nothing else for you.

*

Scene. Looking over her shoulder. Grey-greens and browns. Vague ache of memory subsiding. The dead lamb in the foreground. Middle distance of field and hedgerow. Trees on the horizon. *Hold.*

*

Some time later. Her climbing back over the field-gate and continuing onwards. Colours more muted than before.

*

Elliptical thoughts. The touch of a lover on her shoulder. A bird feigning a broken wing. A hand held in the middle of the night as lightning fills the sky. Blinking back tears. A salt taste in the mouth.

*

Where do they live, these memories, newly risen? Do they thrash around on the surface before sinking back into the silt of forgetting?

*

Ephemeroptera. Those nymphs that lie on the beds of rivers, sometimes for years, before rising to a brief, ecstatic, winged existence. Those clouds of life, catching the sun's light at dusk. And then gone.

III

Shift. An interval of unknown duration. Her, half framed by the road and the sky. An interloper to each.

*

An obstruction in the road. A massive oak tree. *Close up of boughs and branches*. It is not wind damaged or uprooted, but simply leans low over the tarmac as if it has grown that way.

*

Oak means nothing to her. It is a dead word, like those before it. *Yek, yak, eik, āk, ac, aik.* Each of them the mulch of years gone. But there is something else, rising mutely through currents of soil. Anamnesis. The shapes of the leaves, the scent of them. A language beyond language, which speaks to the blood, to the heart.

*

Her scrambling though the tree. Her soft skin against the roughness of bark. Her mere three decades against its countless centuries. And some of the branches catch her face. A wounding caress. See her. Remember her pained eyes. Her intake of breath.

*

On the other side of the tree, an abandoned car. Driven across the ditch and up the steep banks. A futile effort of sheer force and speed. What level of urgency, of fear, would lead someone to try such a thing?

*

She calms herself, absently touching her skin where the branches have marked her. Unease. Colours more vivid. Noise of birds in distance.

*

Long view. The smallness of this encounter against the brute, empty vastness of the north. A bright point amid darkness.

*

Sense of self dilating. Sudden weariness. Dryness of mouth.

*

She approaches the car and sees that the keys are still in the ignition. The vehicle is marooned, useless, but she takes the keys and opens the boot. Faint hope that something else has been left. A spare tyre, some rags and tools. Nothing she can use. Quiet now. She walks on. Into the tide of fear that swept the driver away in the opposite direction.

IIII

.

A farmhouse. Not half a mile from the abandoned car. The last of her provisions eaten she knocks on the door, cautiously at first, then more strongly. Nothing. She walks around the side, looking through the windows. Tries the back door. Open. She shouts hello and is met with silence. The kitchen is in disarray, but there is food here. She quickly prises open a small tin of processed meat and spoons some into her mouth with her fingers. The rest she empties onto a plate, which she consumes with a glass of water. Her hunger abating she moves into the living room. After days on the road it is vaguely exotic to be indoors. More than that, there is a voyeuristic thrill to it. Standing, uninvited, in someone else's home. But there is evidence of panic here. A lampshade lies broken on the floor by the window and the coffee-table is on its side, its glass cracked. Climbing the stairs she calls out again. Still nothing. Go back.

*

A small bedroom at the top of the stairs. Tableau of violence and its attendant fear. Claustrophobic, city fear. A churning sickness in the stomach. Acid rising in the throat. The taste of food in the mouth suddenly obscene before this strange, bloody statue with only half a face. Patron saint of suicides.

*

She kneels without knowing why. The blood in her own body seeming to rush towards her extremities, as if an occult magnetism requires it to join with this other's, this dark glut across the walls and ceiling.

*

On the floor beside the body is a photograph in a gilt frame. A family portrait. Mother, father, daughter. The mother is roughly the same age as her own.

*

This moment. Her eyes again. Clenched hands. Low thrumming like the house itself has awoken. Slant grey light from the window crossing her face, her lips. She begins to shake uncontrollably, mouthing a prayer she hasn't spoken in decades, the words like faded tyre-tracks on the road.

*

And she is watching herself remove the rifle from the dead woman's hands. Lifting her body onto the bed. Wrapping her in its sheets. She is watching herself speak, the voice alien. 'I do not know your name, but I cannot leave you here.'

*

Outside. Low light. She finds a spade in a brick outbuilding. Behind the farmhouse is a field. She begins digging. The soil black, wet and yielding. She digs until she strikes a lighter near-impenetrable layer of subsoil about three feet down. The day is beginning to darken. Back in the house she shoulders the woman's body. It takes all her strength, but she manages to half-carry, half-drag her down the stairs and outside, laying her in the rough hollow she has prepared. No prayers. Just the dark, funereal earth. The feel of it. The scent of it. The taste of sweat on her lips.

*

As she finishes filling the hole a heron flies low and straight over the farm and towards the horizon. She watches it until its shape is lost to the sinking sun. *Hold.*

*

And that shape. That invariant trajectory. Shadow of the straightness of the road in the lower reaches of the sky, but cutting across field and hedgerow. Freedom of the air from the tyranny of path and boundary.

*

The shaking returns. A tremor, emanating from beneath her solar plexus. Something deep, tectonic, inside her, shifting. It feels as if her chest will break open.

*

It is getting cold, but she stands on the threshold of the house. Unwilling to enter. And she is looking, not at this door but another. And her hands are a child's hands. And there is screaming coming from within. Bitter, envenomed argument. A man and a woman. A father and a mother.

*

And the image of her mother's face. Her bruises. Her skin always mending. Her eyes. The dying of stars.

*

And this house. Its aftermath of violence. A dissonant note struck, and its resonance felt far off. Long ago. Gouge, shatter, scar, fracture.

*

But she cannot listen now. Will not hear it. Not here. It is too much. She opens the door and walks inside. In the kitchen she finds whisky and drinks straight from the bottle. Hours later and the tremors have dissolved in an alcoholic stupor.

*

Analgesic sleep. Darkness inside the farmhouse. The forms of things lost to themselves.

*

At some point in the night she wakes with a start and grips the rifle to her chest. Quiet for the longest time. Nothing but her heart, her breathing, her darkness. And then a long, shrill scream. Other than human. Somewhere beyond the house but not far. Not far enough. She struggles to her feet in the lightless room and feels her way to the back door. As silently as she can she makes her way out into the yard. Another scream, more visceral in its nearness. A sudden metallic taste in her mouth. There. On the roof of the outhouse. The pale form of an owl. Its cordate face and its preternatural eyes. It hisses a greeting and her blood runs thready in response.

*

This thought. Childhood stories about owls, about how seeing or hearing them is meant to presage death, and how they are supposed to claim the souls of the just-departed. Here, in the boundless dark, beneath the stars' fullness, none of this seems fanciful. She stands as long as she can in the cold, brimming air. Nothing but the here and now. And it is everything.

*

Later. Her trying to sleep. Dark glut of images. Animals with twisted limbs, falling in and out of life. Deer, their bodies dwindled to nothing, their eyes swollen, pregnant, staring. Eventually, dream. The road's knife drawn along the skin of fields. Blood, rising up through soil, black in the moonlight. A sky, heavy with turning stars. And one star motionless. The pivot, about which all else moves.

*

Morning. Her sitting at the kitchen table. The rifle and a half-full box of cartridges, salvaged from the floor of the suicide room. That city fear, hovering at the threshold of her vision.

*

Outside. She practises her aim in the yard. The rifle is heavy, difficult to hold. When she releases the trigger the butt kicks hard in her shoulder and the sound stuns her. Ears ringing. It seems to reverberate across the broad flatness of the world. Stupid. If there is anyone here I have just announced myself.

V

And that gunshot. Emanating outwards. Across fields, along the lengths of walls and ditches, catching in leaves and branches, shaking birds into the air. Impact of violence to add to all the others. Gouge, shatter, scar, fracture. A sound to wake the dead.

*

Is there anyone here? Yes, there are many. Clamouring for their stories to be heard. Flattened between the pages of earth. Consider this one, for example. A boy, the eldest of four children. Seven born, two dead in the cot and one drowned, a not uncommon fate for children in those days. See him. *Close on his face.*

*

He lives in the lost reaches of this backcountry. A small plot on the fringes of a raised bog of ancient provenance, known locally as the Moss. It was formed from the great proglacial lake, from silt and clay, and the slow lives and suspended deaths of vegetation, of sphagnum and the millennial accumulation of peat. Ten thousand years to raise itself from bedrock, from the harrowed scour of retreating ice.

*

His dozen years held against that vastness and all its knowing. Its deep, unfathomable catalogue of time. But his quick of life, for all that. His bright, burning filament. Self luminous.

*

See him, now, at his mother's side in their low, damp, stone cottage. Her pregnant again and near term, and the father recently dead, leaving them in paupery. And the mother is crying with pain. Something is terribly wrong. It isn't yet her time but she is bleeding, and he hasn't the skill with medicine to stop it. And so he sends a sister for the local healer, two miles away, but it is too far, too late.

*

The child comes, stunted and stillborn, but the mother is dying from an unlocatable haemorrhage. Delirious with blood loss she raves, not about family, or love, or the brevity and futility of life, but the afterlife of the Moss. An incoherent stream of words that the boy cannot fathom. He tries to comfort her, to placate her, to tell her that help is at hand if only she can hang on. And then her trembling body stills and her eyes fix him in a stare, and she says something he will always remember, barely a whisper. 'Burn my body, burn it, don't leave me to him, promise me.'

*

And the healer comes and tends to the body, ushering them all out of the house. All except the boy. And the mother's skin is marked by a creeping black stain that none of the healer's ointments can remove. It seems to emanate from her throat and from an old scar on her side. The healer wraps the body in a winding sheet and tells the boy to quickly prepare a grave. And the boy protests, but he is a boy after all and so ignored. And he cries as he digs the pit. Cries in anger and confusion.

*

And before it is finished the grave is already puddled with bog water, seeping in from the sides. And the body laid there, and the winding sheet stained black, soaking it all up. And he cries and cries, inconsolable. *Promise me*, she had said. *Promise me.*

V I

Vignette of her walking down the road, carrying the rifle. *Close on her face.* Tense, expectant.

*

Moods. Abstract grief. Small terror in pit of stomach. Tremor of leaves in wind.

*

Afterthought. I have lit a candle and surely the moths will come. She walks quickly, putting distance between herself and the farmhouse, all the while listening intently. Watching the tree-line for movements. Proneness of this small female body under the sky's vast canopy.

*

Is it my hearing or does the world seem quieter than yesterday? Is this how it ends? A slow, mute strangulation.

*

Her walking, approaching midday. A diffuse glow in the sky overhead. Some faint memory of sun, of brightness. Try as she might to resist, she cannot help glancing over her shoulder, down the road. Vagrant sense of something following in her wake. A stain, creeping across field, hedgerow and woodland. Touching everything, bleeding into everything. Nothing immune.

*

Afternoon. It occurs to her only now that she is carrying an incriminating weapon. That she has left her trace in a house of blood. Why had she buried that stranger? Would her compassion be interpreted by others as guilt? But which others, exactly? This a world in which the usual rules are suspended.

*

She tries to think of the last time she heard a police siren, or any noise of traffic or human life for that matter. A helicopter, many days ago, low to the south. Had she discovered the suicide in ordinary circumstances she would have notified the authorities, waited to give her testimony, and left. A latent witness, nothing more. But here, she felt compelled to involve herself. The thought of that poor woman decomposing in such a familial setting had been too much to bear, and so she had acted. But was an unmarked grave any improvement? Why do we hide things away in the earth, when they can remain hidden only for so long? Perhaps it is simply the hiding that is enough. And here I am, hiding myself. Running away like a thief.

*

Thinking of how she had performed those last rites with dutiful care it shames her to realise how often she had previously turned a blind eye to so much suffering. I do not know your name, but I cannot leave you here. And yet with great relief she had left her own mother in a care home. Had abandoned the person with whom she'd had the most sustained relationship of her life. And the visits had become less and less frequent. And now she cannot remember the date of their last meeting.

*

As exposed as she feels, out here on the road, something within her wants to scream aloud. To draw out those presences that flutter at the dim edges of her vision. Despite the silence there is a fullness in the air. A sense of concealed, watchful agency.

*

Some hours later, on the threshold of hearing, an unfamiliar sound. Down the road somewhere. Far off, but persistent. A nagging static at the fringes of silence. Be careful what you wish for.

*

Colours. Blue-green, blue-brown, blue-grey. Veins beneath skin.

*

As she walks the sound becomes more audible. Eventually, this. Something in pain or great distress. A kind of yelping, a pitiful whining. She runs.

*

It comes from beyond a small copse of trees at a bend in the road. A white picture-postcard bungalow with a red door and window frames. A garden to the front. Flowers, hanging baskets, shrubbery, but no signs of any occupants.

*

Sensations. Heart in throat. Tightness of chest. Sudden sharp pain in fingers. Her rubbing them, absently.

*

Sound from small byre to rear of cottage. Shallow scraped depression in dirt beneath door. Barely a few centimetres deep. And something pawing at it. Desperately trying to scratch its way out. A dog. The door itself chained shut.

*

Who would leave an animal chained, starving it to death? At the sound of her voice the whine suddenly transforms itself into a demented, high-pitched barking. She speaks again and again, softly, soothingly.

*

In the yard she finds an iron rod and tries to prise the lock chain apart. She leans on it with all her weight, and all the while the dog barking and whining. I'm here, I'm here, I'm here. But the chain is simply too strong and she can't force it open.

*

In desperation she picks up a large stone, raises it over her head and brings it down on the lock. The dog squeals, as if it too has been struck. Again and again she brings the stone down hard. Finally the lock gives way and the door falls open. The animal was clearly kennelled here when the cottage was inhabited. There is bedding and a now-empty food bowl. There is also a large metal trough that looks just about empty of water. She has arrived just in time. The whole place reeks of urine. The dog itself, a grey-white border collie, cowers and snarls. Ears flattened, tail tucked between its legs. It has one blue eye and one brown. A merle.

*

She backs out slowly, all the while speaking to it gently.

*

Inside the house she finds little of use, but there are a
few biscuits left inside an ornate willow pattern jar. She
empties them into her hand and then smashes the jar
on the kitchen floor. A futile protest. Outside the dog is
still trembling in the byre. She breaks a biscuit, eats half
herself, and puts the other half on the ground just outside the door, before backing off to a safe distance. After
ten minutes of coaxing the dog finally steps out into the
daylight. It is awfully emaciated. It eats the piece of biscuit, its tail wagging like a broken propeller. She places
another biscuit on the road and backs off some more.

*

And so it continues. Her walking down the road, turning
every hundred yards or so, stooping, and placing another
piece of biscuit on the ground. And the dog following,
always at a safe distance. Always to one side, as close to
the shelter of the verge as possible.

*

Moods. Residual anger. Magnetism. Some small vestige of hope.

*

Towards nightfall. Another abandoned house. That fear again. Mother, father, daughter. What happens when the living and the dead are cognate? How to distinguish them in the dark? She feels the beginnings of the tremors. *Close on her eyes.*

*

Learn something from the straightness of the road. Its singularity. Its purpose. You are safe here. You are safe.

*

The rear door is unlocked. She fumbles inside for a light switch. Alien grey-black anatomy of walls and windows. Unknown expanse of space within, receding into the dark. Sudden high-pitched whine in ears. Night, keep your terrors to yourself.

*

There are matches in her kitbag. She kneels, feeling blindly for them. Seconds, aching.

*

The brief burst of light conjures momentary shapes out of the darkness before it contracts to a dim aura around her hand. The singing in her ears intensifies, her throat pulsing, as if it would hatch a swarm of insects. You are safe here. You are safe.

*

Again and again, the scent of the matches fills the room. Small brightness held against the void. Sibilant flicker of the dead coming back to life.

*

Finally, there. A candle on a sideboard. She lights it, and the room settles, slowly divulging its secrets, its black vastness reduced to meagre quotidian proportions.

*

The lights don't work, but she finds more candles in a kitchen drawer. Scent of carbolic soap and lavender. She edges into each room, a candle thrust out before her, circling, chanting softly to herself. Improvised ritual for the annulment of fear.

*

Annexed to the kitchen is a small cold-room. She places a candle on one of the empty shelves and kneels to examine the contents of some dust-covered boxes on the floor.

*

Scene. Her kneeling, and the candle above her, the room lambent. The look of it, hallowed in its bareness. Shrine to some beggarly god.

*

Outside the merle whines and she cocks her head, listening intently. The noise in her ears diminishing to a background hum.

*

One of the boxes holds a collection of delicate cups and saucers. Family relics. The bones of saints. Sudden image of her mother's face, her eyes pooling with tears. Stab of pain at her shoulder blades.

*

The other smaller box contains canned meat and pasta shells. Emergency rations. Give thanks.

*

She puts wood in the stove and soon the house is warm and a pan of water is boiling. She calls the merle, speaks to it gently, but, still wary of doors, it loiters outside. Hunched down in the growing dark. She empties half a tin of meat onto a saucer and takes it into the yard. The dog snarls and backs off at first, but only a foot or so, before quickly devouring the meal and licking the plate clean. She brings water and biscuits and speaks to it as night gathers the horizon to itself. 'Tell me again why I am doing this? We can stay here, can't we? We have each other. You'll like me in time.'

*

She can't coax the animal inside any further than the kitchen, and so she makes her bed on the floor beside it. Although exhausted she cannot sleep, her whole body pulsing, trembling. Through the window the stars are imperceptibly circling, performing their own circadian rituals against the blackness of night.

*

Shift. She has spent the day bringing in wood from an outbuilding and scouring the vicinity for food. In a house two miles away she has found provisions for a week or more. Tins of meat and tuna. Oats. Flour and oil. She has even found dog food.

*

In the evening she lights a fire. The merle has spent the day close to her, and now it sits by her feet. Sometimes the animal looks up at her with such expression in its face. Here is language of a different order. She feels something reach out between them in the fire light. Is this how the age-old bond between humans and wolves was formed? The sharing of food. Eye contact. Warmth. I will never hurt you.

*

Later. As the fire embers, her mind drifts. Again that dark glut of images, seeming to fissure up inside her. Yet there is something else. An undertow, a cloying feeling, shadowing her steps these past days. A sense of suffocation, kept in abeyance, so at odds with the openness and emptiness of this backcountry. And now, on the threshold of sleep, it seizes her.

*

Dream. She is bound in throttling darkness. Confined so tightly she cannot move her arms. And something cold and wet and unspeakably old presses against her. And she screams and chokes. Her mouth filling with viscous silt liquid, which she swallows and swallows and takes down into her. Her stomach sick. And the feeling of her body filling, bloating, transfiguring into something other. And all the while voices. A murmuring chorus. Chthonic. Hideous.

*

She wakes gasping, clutching at her neck. And in these aching moments the darkness of the room and the darkness of her dream are one. And the voices she hears only slowly transpose themselves into the whine of the dog by her feet. And now the feel of it licking her hand. The warmth of it. 'Don't leave me,' she whispers. 'Please don't leave.'

*

And the next night the same, and the night after that. But the following night, this. She sees a hollow in a vast marsh, filled with water. Feels many hands upon her. A rope put around her neck and tightened until she cannot breathe. A sharp pain in her side. And then she is thrust into the cold, dark water, where she is drowned. But this is not the worst of it. This not the end of it. For in that dank pool she sees a body rise up to meet her, and its hands take hold of her. A man's unyielding grip. And his skin is stained the colour of the earth itself. His face staring, eyeless. And though dead she struggles and struggles. But he is too strong, and he pulls her close. A crushing embrace. And they sink down together.

*

And as she wakes at the limits of her terror she knows that they cannot stay. This place is a snare. A bloody and painful trap. They must continue onwards. Down the road.

VII

Early morning. The boy is lying in bed. Slant light across his face. Closed eyes. But his thin film of sleep is pierced by unusual sounds from behind the cottage. He creeps outside and ventures quietly among the trees. Seven men standing around the grave. They have uncovered the body and are hammering long willow stakes into her hands and feet. Without thinking he charges at them, screaming. Two of the men catch him, pin him down and cover his mouth, whilst the others continue at their work in silence. 'Don't make us come back for you, boy,' one of them says as they leave. 'I knew your father. He would have done the same for any of us. You'll know it better when you're grown.'

*

His father, already beneath the earth. No use to the living.

*

Shift. The bleed of days into each other. Whereas before he had floated in fitful sleep, he now sinks into something deeper, more terrifying. In its darkness he sees visions of her, her flesh the colour of the earth, her long golden hair turned root black. She looks nothing like the mother he remembers, but he knows it is her. The pendant about her neck, a figurine made of bog oak, he has known from his earliest days. Her body is perforated by a cage of willow stakes and her eyes spill from their sockets like star jelly. 'Free me,' she says wordlessly. 'You must free me. You can't leave me like this. This is yours to fix.'

*

Close on him. Shaking in his bed, trying not to wake the others. See him. His eyes. One blue and one brown. Primal terror of the known world made strange. *Hold.*

*

The dream continues, night after night, until he is driven to thoughts of suicide. In his desperation he visits the healer to confess his condition, and she gives him a tincture of valerian, hops and oats to take each evening. For weeks to follow his dreams are a caliginous sediment, and he is thankful.

*

But during his days he begins to have the sensation of an unwanted presence at the threshold of his senses. Something rupturing, fissuring up, spilling inside him.

*

One bright afternoon he is out on the Moss, turning the
stacked peat that is drying on their familial plot. As he
gathers his shoes to leave he hears his name spoken and
turns to see her standing an arm's distance away. So real
he reaches out to touch the empty air.

*

That night he uncovers his mother's corpse, removes the
rods of willow that pin her to the earth, and lifts the pendant from around her neck. There is no wood for a pyre,
and so, in desperation, he empties their winter store of
parrafin over her body and sets her alight.

*

The fire blazes briefly and fiercely, but soon enough the fuel is spent and her corpse emerges from the smoke, merely blackened. He is shaking uncontrollably. But then the sound of his youngest sister crying in the house jolts him into action, and he quickly infills the grave. I can do nothing else for you.

VIII

Early morning. The woman and the merle and the road. The muted sound of footfall against the brash silence of field and distant woodland.

*

Close on her face in the pale, far-off sunlight. The beginnings of shadows around her eyes.

*

That feeling again, pressing behind her. Perhaps, after days moving along these pale corridors of the north, she is finally sensing its penumbra of violence. Attrition and gravity. Blood and water. Slow vastness. Gouge, shatter, scar, fracture.

*

Asemia. Great cryptic scrawl of passing trees. Dense lines of hedgerow and undergrowth. Impenetrable mass of cognate forms. As if an unknown hand has written the same tangled glyphs over and over and over.

*

And so her thoughts return again to the woman she had buried. The bloodied mess of her body, now lying beneath soil. How many others? Nothing is truly hidden.

*

She continues onwards. Pain in her feet and ankles. See her. Her skin. Her clenched hands. The straightness of the road a prayer.

*

From one body beneath the earth to another. That eyeless face. What disease of mind could affect her dreams so tangibly? What latent pathology has this sleeping greygreen world awakened within her?

*

Spiralling thoughts of illness. She had watched her own mother fall slowly into dementia at an age that was too young for them both. It always frightened her to think of it. To think of heredity. Matrilineality. This I leave to you, daughter. The loss of me, but also the loss of yourself, in time. A blade with two edges, the first sharp, the second dull, but somehow more cutting.

*

Over the past few years her mother had become increasingly mired in compulsive thoughts, unable to free herself. She would walk, somehow escaping the vigilance of neighbours, and strand herself beyond the limits of her internal map. Eventually a wristband with an emergency contact number was procured, but like a cat with a new collar she would uncouple herself from it. A last defiance. The expression of a certain form of freedom as the condition stripped her of others. But eventually she even acquiesced to this, no longer seemed to even notice it. In hindsight this should have been taken as a sign.

*

And more and more often the phone's ring signalled the voice of another stranger who had found her mother wandering the street where she was born, knocking at each door, unable to find the house in which she had spent her young life because it was no longer there. Demolished to make way for the new.

*

The image of her mother's face, tearful and confused. Are our minds like the land? Bounded. A limited territory.

*

A tide had visited her mother's world, washing away the new-built, the insubstantial, the profane, to reveal in vivid detail the obdurate foundations of her childhood. By contrast her daughter could conjure little of her own former life in the north. Was it only the rupture of disease or trauma that could bring those deeper memories to the surface? Had she yielded to that voice calling her here because this journey back to the places of her young life presented the opportunity to walk her own boundaries, to see what memories returned to her, and what clung to the obstinate earth?

*

Her walking is laboured now. Approaching day's end. Faint churr of birds against the dimming sky. Tightness in her chest. Occluded thoughts. Low islands of reason.

*

She finds shelter as the light begins to turn. A farmhouse at the end of a winding driveway. The utter loneliness of it. The orphaned familial pictures on the walls. The drawers of trinkets and bric-a-brac. The much cared-for ornaments, now forsaken. How can you go on? Why endure? You have been discarded, forgotten.

*

Such is her fatigue that she sleeps almost immediately. Can no longer fight that pull, dragging her downwards.

*

In the half-light of dream she sees the eyes of those who are to drown her. Sees their fear, their sallow cheeks, their hunger for death and rebirth. Bright frenzy at the edge of their gazing. And her mouth is burning from the gruel that is their first and last kindness. Milk boiled with honey, barley, yarrow, starwort, and a dozen other plants. Milk turning black with the taint of peat-water spilling inside her. Bones and organs dissolving. And all the while singing. Song of the ending, and the endless beginning. Now it is your turn.

*

When she regains the room it is still echoing with her screaming, and she feels at her throat and knows at last that she is in the land of the living. And she cries and cries, and says her thanksgivings.

*

But later, when she has lit candles and chased as much of the dark away as she can, and when her thoughts have finally exhausted themselves, still one remains. Unshakeable. This time I awoke here, in this museum of the forgotten, but soon enough I will wake in blackness under the earth. And there will be no more dreaming.

*

She does not know of Grauballe, of Tollund, of Cashel. She does not know of the great constellation of inhumations scattered across northern Europe. She does not know of the triple death. Of overkill. Of the sanctity and afterlife of peat and water. But this she remembers, rising slowly up through the mire of her own biography. A voice. A man's voice. Gentle. *There are things buried here. Things whose oldness you can only guess at. Do you dream? There is someone, a man, and he is at the centre. He is the pivot, about which all else moves. He is here, buried. Do you dream?*

*

And she recognises at last the sensation from the depths of her childhood. Yes, she had dreamed. Yes, she had experienced this dream before. Death, and its absolution in marsh water. And those narrow rooms beneath. Those myriad unseen channels. The writhing mass of consciousnesses. Yes, she had been there.

*

And the choking terror of those nights. The sweats. The bed-wetting. The screams that would wake her mother. And the fear and impotence in her mother's voice. 'It's alright, love. It's alright. I'm here now. No one's going to hurt us.'

VIIII

He is fifteen now. The first flush of manhood in him. He has grown over the last summer and feels a strength and pliancy in his limbs like the young birch trees on the edge of the Moss. A girl he has known since childhood from the south side has grown too. And now when he sees her he lowers his gaze, frightened. And the look in her eyes as she passes him in the communion line more holy than benediction.

*

His dreams now, full of her, her voice, the shape of her body. The longing of youth, a fire by the waters of adulthood. Revel in it, though it burns the skin.

*

And somehow they overcome the clumsiness of speech, the foreignness of their own bodies, and begin to meet each other out on the Moss, away from watchful eyes.

'If only they knew I was meeting you,' she tells him, 'they'd kill me.'

'Don't say that.'

'I mean, they say your mother was a witch.' She knows instantly that she has wounded him. She reaches out to touch him, and he yields. Somehow they both know that this is the first of many wounds to come, and that the gentle pressure of each other's bodies can heal them. And so she holds him. And the taste of her in his mouth more sacred than the flesh of any god.

*

And he gives her his only possession of any value. The pendant he has worn since his mother's reinterment. Places it around her neck. Its charcoal blackness against the whiteness of her skin.

*

As their intimacy grows she jokes that she will become his protectress. His witch. No sting in those words now. Love has given them a new meaning.

*

She is apprentice to the healer, and as they walk among the birch, alder and pine at the edge of the Moss she tells him the worth of things. Birch leaf for rheumatism, bog moss for dressing wounds, club moss for dropsy, peat tar an antiseptic.

*

'What about these?' he asks, flourishing a small spray of tansy flowers that he has gathered from the garden of a neighbouring farm.

'They're beautiful,' she says, 'but we use them for worms, and for other things.'

'Other things?'

'If a woman doesn't want her baby.'

There is something odd in her voice as her eyes fix on the mass of water and earth before them.

'You mean?' He flushes, then plucks the flowers from her hand and throws them into a nearby pool in the Moss.

'Why did you do that?' There is an edge to her voice.

'I didn't know what they were for.'

'Please don't do that,' she says. 'Don't ever take back a gift. It's bad luck.'

'I'm sorry.'

She kisses him, but she cannot stop trembling.

X

Scene. The woman and the merle. Down the road. Tableau of straight grey asphalt and the spilling, spiralling green of verge. Tension of grey and green. Enmity of civilisation and of earth.

*

Blunted sameness of land and sky. Nothing sharp. Nothing memorable. Blurred focus of the world. Have I not always been here? Passing the same fields, trees, walls. Over and over and over.

*

But that voice. His voice. Pressing at her temples. A bird feigning a broken wing, drawing her not away from its nest but towards it. Towards something. Where are you leading me? Is there an end in sight?

*

Later. Another crossroad. Another illusion of choice. She hesitates. Looks up and down. Listens. Minutes pass. There. Distant, faint. That deep, guttural sound. Emanating from the far woods to the north.

*

Luminous eyes. Seven tines on each antler. Do you shadow me, or do I shadow you?

*

She takes the north road and begins walking, but the merle is whining behind her. She turns. The dog stands, unmoving, at the crossroad.

*

Memory. Her tending to her mother in a garish room. The walls' brightness against the dulling of her mother's mind. She lifts her arm to comb the other's hair. Small gesture of intimacy, of care. But her mother sees finger-shaped bruises on her forearm, and there is suddenly something rising within the older woman, coming to her surface. A charm for the annulment of fear. 'He's gone. He's gone.' It is barely a whisper, but there is venom in it, and a look the daughter will never forget breaks across the mother's face, before sinking back within her. Traceless.

*

She blinks, scanning the horizon to the north. Oblique afterimage of something metallic and sharp-edged, hidden in the long grass of a far-off field. A faint choking feeling in the throat.

*

She kneels and calls gently to the merle, and only after minutes of coaxing does it finally relent, and they walk on together.

*

Miles on the road, or so it seems. And the road itself narrowing even further. Beginning to green. A cold dampness in the air.

*

Eventually a low stone cottage, the front gate open and the lawn scattered with household objects. Books. Ornaments. Clothing. All discarded in the rush to salvage only the essentials. It looks as if the house itself has coughed them up. The undigested remnants of its last meal.

*

By the path a child's doll. She kneels to pick it up. Stark impression in the grass beneath it. A coldness between her shoulders. Slowly spreading up her neck and down her back. Quiet. As if everything is holding its breath.

*

And again her hands are a child's hands. The doll, hers. The low stone cottage, her childhood home. And there are ghosts of violence moving among the disarray inside.

*

She stands, a girl in the shatter of broken plates on the kitchen floor, and calls and calls for her mother. Daylight fading into the last night on earth. And only later does her mother return, the skin around her eyes discoloured, swollen. Her shoes wet and caked in mud, and the father gone, nowhere to be seen.

*

Colours. Heightened. Blue of kitchen cabinets. Yellow of wallpaper. Fridge adorned with rainbows of child's scribbles.

*

How to be here? How to continue remembering, when each memory is a wound?

*

She is hungry but cannot eat. A sickness rising from the depths of her stomach. She feeds the merle and lights a fire, before lying down to rest on the settee in the front room.

*

Dream. A train carriage, empty except for a man with a stranger's face sitting some distance behind her. Her wanting so badly to get off the train, but feeling compelled to stay, unable to leave this man whom she knows and yet does not know. Water pooling beneath his feet. And the journey endless, and through the windows the forms of ruined buildings, engulfed by plants and trees, slipping past her at high speed. Not another person in sight. And her wanting so badly to get off the train.

*

Later. A primal sense jolting her awake. And in the blackness of the room the shape of something darker. High beating of her heart. The house, thrumming, alive. Her fumbling for the rifle. Aching slowness of hands in the dark. A warning shot. Blinding brightness.

*

Her ears ringing. Her scouring the dark room for a candle. Struggling to light it, hands trembling.

*

And it is only now that she notices the merle is gone. Frightened by the gunshot. And despite the dark, and the danger, she would call to it, but she does not know its name. In impotent fury she screams at the night. And deep within the dark fields of her childhood, an echo, an answer. A girl's grieving cry.

*

Morning. She waits in the cottage, hoping the merle will return. There is a newspaper on the kitchen table, and she flicks through it distractedly. War and unrest in far-flung places. Disease. Corruption. Genocide. Gyres of plastic in the ocean. Fires in the forests of the world. I am a spoke in a great and infernal wheel.

*

As day reaches its full, meagre brightness she scours the adjacent fields. There is a small derelict byre in the far corner of one field, but the soft soil around it is undisturbed, and there are no signs of the merle inside. Remembering the animal's reluctance at the crossroad she retraces their steps. It takes hours, and there is nothing. No sign of her companion.

*

Close on her face, eyes. Birdsong and drying tears. Centre of the vortex of her suffering. Bright pain of loss against the dull stranding of her reason.

*

By the time she makes it back to the cottage it is late afternoon. Last hope of finding the merle inside, but the house is empty. Sickness of hunger and of despair. She scours the house but finds nothing edible. All that remains in her provisions is a half-packet of biscuits. It is reckless, perhaps, but she will not stay here another night.

*

Useless vision. Useless touch. Low, worn engines of time. Dead scatter of stars. The world itself, bloodless. Abandoned. No way back.

*

Outside. Her against the road, the trees, the fields, the sky. Vague self-hatred of existence. *Colours.* Darkening. Blue-grey, blue-green, blue-brown.

*

Every few hundred yards she stops to look back, leaving a piece of biscuit in the road. Vain hope that her lost companion will follow. A breadcrumb trail into this new darkness.

X I

'It's bad luck,' she had said. He turns the words over and over as he waits. Stones, glistening from the river. As day darkens it is clear that she is not coming. This the third time she has broken their promise.

*

He visits the healer, but the girl hasn't been seen in days. The beginnings of fear, rising from the depths of his stomach.

*

He can think of nothing else, and so he sets off for the south side of the Moss. They say your mother was a witch. Those words stinging as fresh as the first time he heard them.

*

He takes a shortcut across fields, the soft earth sucking at his feet. These grassed enclosures, stolen from the wetlands through a network of drains, have always been sluggish. Prone to sedges and rushes. They have never thrived, never flourished, as if the water, long ago, had cursed them for its banishment. And so timber quickly turns to rot, metal to rust. The green of things always seeming leached, as if ash were the major constituent, and not chlorophyll.

*

Eventually, a house shaded by a stand of birch trees. *Colours.* Bone-white of the birch against a background of greens and browns. Dull gunmetal grey of the house. Red trim to the windows, a gash of brightness. He has barely stepped on the driveway before the front door opens. A man, the father, emerges, holding a rifle. The sound of crying emanating from within. *Her.*

*

The man speaks with the gun. A single report that the boy feels, close to his ear, before the sound reaches him. It seems to reverberate across the broad flatness of the world. Gouge, shatter, scar, fracture.

*

He takes one last look at the house. Sees her face in the window. Another shot explodes on the driveway near his feet. He turns and he runs.

XII

Her walking, footsore, weary. Attrition of road, of thought. Fear is fear, violence is violence. All men's hands are the same.

*

That question again. How to be here? The fields would tell her, if she would but listen. The here and now a reprieve, a moment between concussions. Millennia as seconds. Greenness an effort. Great skin of the world always mending. Time over time.

*

Gouge, shatter, scar, fracture. And so narcoma will become the new god.

*

Early evening. Smoke rising not far down the road. Thinly scratched symbol in the sky. *Come.* She stops, fear coiling around her neck. She looks up and down the road. Go back? There is nothing for it but onwards.

*

She approaches, heart hammering. 'Is there anyone there?' she asks. After the quiet of the road her voice seems unnaturally loud. Some moments later a man emerges. Her whole body goes cold. He is thin beneath several layers of clothes, older, perhaps mid-to-late thirties, and drags his right foot behind the other. He slowly makes his way towards her, squinting with his neck craned forward. When he is about six feet away she gestures with the rifle for him to stop. He blinks, apparently seeing the weapon for the first time, raising his hands in alarm. His face is that of a man who does not sleep, and it frightens her.

*

They stand in uncomfortable silence. Seconds, aching.
A sweet smell to his unwashed body. At last he turns,
gesturing for her to follow.

*

They walk through a narrow yard and past an old wooden
dwelling. Stacked by its ornately carved doorway are
an assortment of log baskets crafted from willow, all
filled with wood. The campfire is burning nearby. They
continue into an adjacent field where he beckons her
towards a large oak tree.
'It was dead. Hadn't put out leaves in years.' He licks his
lips before speaking. His hand visibly trembling as he
points. 'I was going to cut it down for the fire.'
Among the leaves are dozens of small figures. Stick
people, cut out of thin strips of metal and tied to the
branches. He sees her eyes lingering on them as they
glint in the low sunlight. He gestures at them, his mouth
moving, searching for words. But there are none.

*

His ashen face. His stooped posture. Years of sunless mornings compacted in the air around him. She shifts uneasily.

*

'Where are you making for?' he asks. There is a stutter to his voice. It is clear that he hasn't spoken to anyone in some time. The words are coming back to him only slowly.

'I'm not sure.' She points back to the road. 'I used to live up around here, somewhere, when I was little.'

He raises an eyebrow. 'What's your name, your family name?'

*

She wavers, on the brink of telling, thinking about the burden of names, and of belonging. She wavers, and then she tells him, and it is like casting a tiny quartz pebble into a vast, placid lake. It ripples over his face and he blinks, seeming to see her for the first time. He brings a hand to his forehead and it is only then that she notices his arm is marked with cuts, all quite recent, some barely healed.

'I know that name. Maybe I've seen it on maps of the Moss.'

*

The Moss. The word is alien, and yet suddenly familiar. He sees the ambivalence in her face. 'You know it, surely? The marsh, a few miles north of here.'

*

How to speak of dreams as if they are real? The ground feels momentarily unstable beneath her feet, like she might sink and fall.

*

'And your name?' she asks finally.

He tells her. Small spasm of recognition.

'Are you from here too?'

'Yes, on my father's side.' His voice is bruised, hesitant. He draws a deep breath. 'Now that we're introduced,' he bows slightly, 'come have some food. It's getting late.'

*

She watches him turning tins of vegetables in the camp-fire. Whilst he does so he mutters to himself, the words lost to the flames. A vagrant benediction. The care with which he turns the tins makes it seem like a ritual from the long-lost past. The palm of one of his hands, she notices, is marked with newly healed cuts in concentric circles. A bloody rewriting of the lines of fate, life and of the heart. A chiromancy for a future age.

*

He deals her the largest portion and they sit and eat in silence. She can barely take a mouthful. Something in this gesture of sharing food, here, at the end of the world, moves her beyond normal feeling. After he finishes eating he stares into the fire for countless minutes. His head moving up and down slowly, his jaw jutting in and out, as if trying to start a broken motor. It finally catches, and he turns to her. His eyes luminous in the firelight. 'Do you dream?'

*

Waves, crashing against her shore. She cannot speak, but nods, her eyes lowered. Moments pass. She flicks a glance at him. He nods too, smiling grimly, and returns his gaze to the fire. She feels a spark of sympathy, of intimacy, leap between them. Who are you, Prince of Scars, and why do you stay here, at this bitter outpost, when all others have deserted?

*

They speak no more about it. This simple, wordless acknowledgement is all that seems necessary. But she cannot get warm despite the heat. There is a coldness in her depths. The coldness of water.

*

They talk brokenly of other things, and as evening slowly turns to night, they fall into a rapt silence before the fire.

*

Fire images. The heat seeming to release them, bringing them to her surface like a poultice. Her skin prickling, feverish, even if her bones are cold. *Her mother's tearful face. Stones arranged on a window sill. A lamb with deformed forelegs. A path through a field, leading to a marsh. Treacherous, sodden ground. Water, drowning. A hand on her wrist, pulling her out of the mire. The silhouette of a man. A night sky, brimming with stars.* Each image begetting another. Each image tinged with the same fiery heat.

*

Later. The fire embering, his voice gently breaks her reverie.

'You're going there, I think.'

Silence.

'The Moss. That's where you're headed?'

'I'm not sure.'

*

The silhouette of a man. A night sky, brimming with stars. And one star, its motionless centre.

*

That coldness, swelling in her. Waves of remembrance. Words as fluid rupture, seeking the surface. Pressing at her skin.

*

'There was a man. A kind man. He saved me.' She pauses, her eyes searching the fire. 'I fell in the marsh when I was a girl and nearly drowned. He saved me. I can't see his face, but I know something happened to him.'

*

Tight, choking feeling in her throat. A silt taste. She is trembling.

*

When she looks up he is staring at her intensely, poised as if to speak, but the words do not come.

'Can you help me?' she asks, finally.

'There's a way across the fields. I can show you in the morning.'

She gestures mutely at the pressing darkness.

'Don't worry. I don't sleep. I'll keep the fire going until then.'

'I don't know that I can sleep either.'

'You're safe. We're both safe, here.'

*

Eventually, despite her best efforts, she feels tiredness begin to overwhelm her. She lies on her back, wrapped in a blanket, and tries to find the fixed star in the night sky above. But the fire is too bright, leaching into the darkness. And her eyes are too heavy.

*

She sees vague forms in the dimness of sleep. Like words in a sister tongue, close to our own, but whose meaning can only be guessed at. When she awakes she can barely remember them, and she is thankful.

*

In the pale morning they share stale biscuits and instant coffee, her body numb where it has been in contact with the earth. She sits, watching him as he works up another stick figure for the tree.

*

When he is finished he takes her to the north end of the field. Points to where the low morning light is tracing a faint path across the next field to a wood on the horizon. 'There's a track through the wood. On the other side is the Moss.'

*

As she makes to leave he takes something from his pocket and presses it into her palm. The small metal figure. And it is only now, in daylight, and in such close proximity, that she notices his eyes. One blue, the other brown. A spasm of pain in her chest. She puts her arms around him and thanks him. He flinches at first, and she can feel his body trembling like an animal.

XIII

The slow, inexorable fading of hours into days, weeks, months. He turns sixteen. The aunt who has stayed with them since shortly after his mother's death returns to her village in the south. He is cut loose.

*

The boy busies himself making repairs to the farm. For the past weeks he has been mending a drystone wall that had fallen in a storm whilst his mother was still alive. In among the heart stones he finds the remains of an old glass jar that must have broken during the wall's collapse. There are iron nails and bits of bone scattered throughout the wreckage. He collects as much of it as he can and takes it back to the cottage. When the others are asleep he gets up and lays each fragment out across the kitchen table, studying them intently in the lamplight. She would know what it is, and what to do with it.

*

Over the intervening months he has tried to get messages to her. In each of them the same words. He will wait for her, once a week, at the place only they know. Out on the Moss.

*

At the appointed hour he waits, as he has countless times before. When she does not appear he remains. A well-practised ritual of diminishing hope. An hour turns into two. All the while he turns one of the glass jar's rusted nails over and over between his fingers. It grows dark and still he waits, pressing the nail harder and harder into the flesh of his palm. The pain somehow erotic, somehow thrilling.

*

When he returns home they are waiting for him.

*

He doesn't say anything and neither do they. He feels their hands on him. A jute bag tied over his head. His body dragged out of the house, lifted and carried who knows where. He doesn't struggle, doesn't scream, but works the nail deeper into his hand. The pain a fire that his mind gathers around in the darkness.

*

When they unmask him they are out on the edge of the
Moss. The scent of it in the air. The feel of it underfoot.
As his eyes accustom to the moonless night he sees that
they are beneath an alder tree. Its trunk is split in two,
like a tuning fork stuck into the earth. On the left-hand
trunk there is a huge burr, which looks like a black eyeless face. And from that trunk there hangs an improvised
noose.

*

The men form a circle around him. One of them, the
girl's father, steps forward, grabs the boy by the neck. His
eyes. The boy's eyes. A grief, unspoken, passing between
them. And then the boy understands. And his world
ends.

*

'The child lives, but you will never see it.'

*

He doesn't feel the knife as it pierces his side. Doesn't feel it as they string him up and watch his body convulse. Feels nothing but the pain in his hand, which has become a kind of ecstasy. And he watches them watching him. Watches them sink into confusion, and then fear.

*

The searing pain continues. At the limits of his consciousness he sees his mother. Sees her still-warm body laid out on her deathbed. That dark venous map contouring her skin, emanating from her throat and the scar on her side. And as his life flickers out he sees her body change and become his beloved. Her milk-white flesh. Her sacred geometry. Dark whorls mottling the skin over her womb.

*

When his body stills they cut him down and throw him in a deep pool out on the Moss. Hold him under for minutes to make sure he is drowned. Weight his body with bags filled with stones from the river. Later they cover the pool with turf so that it looks like any other part of that place. Neither land nor water but something in-between.

XIIII

Her walking through the field towards the wood. The sensation underfoot so different from the hard surety of concrete and asphalt.

*

Thought no longer banked, no longer kept to its meagre runnel, but eddying ever outwards, away from itself. Water merging with water, becoming indistinguishable, seeping below ground.

*

Moods. Wavering. Uncertain. Loss of that road-narrow sight.

*

Something in the yielding softness of grass and moss.
A shift in the rhythm of walking. The consciousness
that each footstep impinges upon something living. Eyes
drawn away from the horizon and towards the feet.

*

Incipient sense that her child's eye had once been atten-
tive to each form, no matter how small or seemingly
insignificant. And the names of each flower once known,
but now forgotten. Each loss an extinction.

*

Scene. Her among trees. Birch, alder, pine. Their forms. Sameness dissolving into difference. Green and brown becoming variegated. Her skin taking on each hue like a taint.

*

Dank, close air. Rot, fungal bloom. Grey-silver of lichen, grey-green of moss. Muted, strangled life of this place of thresholds. Archaic putrescence of the world.

*

A deep, guttural sound rings out in the wood. A cervine shape, somewhere close. But how to see those eyes and antlers among the countless boughs and branches? She is holding her breath.

*

There, again. Further off. Moving to the north. She follows.

*

After a little over a mile she comes to the fenced northern perimeter of the wood. Following it east she finds a stile leading to a narrow road. It is steeply banked on one side and encroached by heavy gorse on the other. As she walks northwards the gorse gives way to beech and lime, and the ditch begins to brim with running water. The road curves to reveal a small whitewashed bungalow, half of its roof caved in by a fallen tree.

*

This moment. Painted wooden door and window-frame of the home she last saw two decades ago and more. Lawn to front, much smaller than she remembers. Driveway to side barely the length of a car. Road bending sharply northwards.

*

Sensations. Hammering of heart in throat. Numbness in lower legs. Dryness of mouth.

*

She approaches the door. It is unlocked. She is a child once more.

*

A commotion inside. Her mother is seated at the kitchen table and there are two others she doesn't recognise. One is a young policewoman and the other an older man. Her mother leaps up and runs to her, holding her close, asking over and over if she is okay. There is whisky on her breath.

*

After the initial euphoria, the tears and kisses, the questions begin. She tells them that she has been out on the Moss and hadn't realised how late it was.
'Who have you been with?'
'No one.'
'Don't worry, you're not in trouble.'
Her tongue feels like a foot in a shoe it has long outgrown. She looks up at the man. He is staring at her. Grey eyes, unreadable.

*

'Did you meet anyone out there?' the mother asks. The policewoman glances remonstratively.

'No.'

'Then who gave you that shawl?'

'No one,' she says, looking at the man again. A pitiless smile plays at the edge of his mouth, his eyes seeming to bore right into her. He knows, she says to herself. He knows.

'It's okay, love,' says the mother. 'We just need to make sure you're okay.'

'I'm fine. There's nothing to tell.'

'But who gave you the shawl?'

'I found it.'

'Don't lie to your mother,' says the man. 'He gave it you, didn't he?'

She cannot look up. Tears in her eyes now.

'Did he touch you, sweetheart?'

'No.'

*

She still cannot look up. Her hands shaking, she pulls the shawl tightly around her throat. The policewoman and the mother exchange glances.

'Look at her clothes. Look at her arm.'

There is a bruise forming where he had grabbed her and pulled her from the marsh, and some scratch marks where his fingernails had inadvertently caught her skin.

'I'll leave you to it,' says the man, standing. 'I've seen enough.'

'Who is he?' the mother asks.

'A willow worker. Queer sort. Lives rough on the south side, penniless. And his boy lame and no mother around.'

The policewoman begins to interject but he cuts her off. 'Something not right about them. Have you seen their eyes?'

*

After he has left they question her for another hour and slowly the truth emerges. She had strayed into an unfamiliar part of the Moss where she had fallen. A man had saved her, carried her away from danger, warmed her before a campfire. But there is a large bruise developing on her inner thigh, and as they press her for more details a silent language of fear moves between the two women. Before the officer leaves she instructs the mother that the girl isn't to bathe, and must be brought to the station the next day to be examined for sexual injuries. When she is gone the mother and daughter cannot speak. Each mired in their own private turmoil. Remote and unknowable to the other.

*

At some point the mother finally leaves her, huddled in her bed, looking out of the window across the fields to the sprawl of the Moss beyond. The girl cradles the shawl like a newly born child and cries bitterly.

*

She wakes at first light. As she surveys the grey, misted fields from her window a great throbbing pain wracks her body. She lies, gasping on her bed, clutching the cloak. Its scent seems to soothe her. She rises and quietly slips out of her room, hoping to leave the house without being noticed, but her mother is in the kitchen. She is seated as before. Her eyes on the locked door as if engaged in some sort of vigil.

*

'I'm here, mum.'

'Yes, yes you are,' she replies, beginning to cry. 'This is all too much. First your father, and now this. What were you doing out there? Have you forgotten?'

*

No. The memories of that night were still her constant companions. The silence of the house on her return from school. The shards of broken plates on the kitchen floor. The aftermath of a violence that walls could not contain, spilling outwards across the fields.

*

And the burnt feeling in her throat after she had called and called for her mother, until the words themselves seemed alien, unutterable. And her mother returning only as night fell, the scent of the Moss thick upon her. And those two words, whispered, over and over, as she held her daughter close. 'He's gone. He's gone.'

*

'It's deathly out there,' the mother continues.

'It's okay, mum. I'm okay.'

'And now this stranger. Preying on young girls.'

'He saved me.'

'You're too young. You don't know the half of it. Promise me you'll never go back there.'

Silence.

'Promise me.'

*

It begins to rain. The phone rings mid-morning and they go to the police station. A kind-faced woman talks to her about cats and clothes and summer whilst putting cold instruments between her legs. The woman then speaks with the mother and the mother weeps again. This time with relief. Meanwhile another woman asks the girl a series of questions. *Did he make you do anything? Did he make you touch him? Did he let you go, or did you escape?*

*

Back at home and her mother will not leave her side.

*

Each hour away from the Moss is a brute agony. In two days school is due to resume after the summer holidays. The world of the classroom seems a distant epoch in time. A fable. And all she can think about are those grey eyes and that pitiless smile.

*

She has to find a way to warn her rescuer. She can't quite express how, but she knows he is in danger. But her mother follows her every step during daylight hours. And the doors and windows are locked and bolted after nightfall.

*

To be trapped. Imprisoned like an animal in a cage. No way to get out.

*

The mother can see how wretched she is. She warms some milk and honey on the stove. Pours it into a mug and gives it to her.
'Drink. It will do you good.'
She drinks, and it is sweet.
'No nightmares tonight,' the mother adds, stroking her hair.

*

Nightmares. Choking terror. *Do you dream?* he had said. She cries again, and her mother gathers her up, tries to comfort her.

'You're safe now,' she whispers, over and over.

*

But there is something in the drink. Within half an hour she is drowsy, and her mother carries her to bed. She sleeps. And there are dreams.

*

A train carriage, empty except for a man with a stranger's face sitting some distance behind her. Her wanting so badly to get off the train, but feeling compelled to stay, unable to leave this man whom she knows and yet does not know. His skin slack, puckered. Water pooling beneath his feet. And the journey endless, and through the windows the forms of ruined buildings, engulfed by plants and trees, slipping past her at high speed. Not another person in sight. And her wanting so badly to get off the train.

*

The first three hours of school the next day are a drip-feed of poison. But as soon as the dinner bell sounds her spirits are raised. Out on the playground she bides her time, waiting for the first inevitable altercation. Boys in her class. Punches thrown. The invigilating teacher drawn to intervene. And during this distraction she makes her escape.

*

The Moss is nearly two miles away to the north and she sets off down the back roads at a run. About half-way there her lungs are on fire and her heart is in her throat. She stops and vomits onto the tarmac, her limbs trembling with sheer exertion.

*

With her pulse still racing she begins again, but more slowly, checking behind her every few hundred yards, keeping to the verge, ready to take cover at the hint of a person or vehicle.

*

The road crosses a bridge and then climbs steeply through trees. She rests again. At the brow of the hill the road runs flat and straight. Broad fields to each side and a low hedgerow. She feels exposed. Proneness of this small child's body under the sky's vast canopy. She comes to a large sandstone farmhouse to her left with a yew tree in the front garden. As she passes the outbuildings someone calls her name. She turns and sees him. Grey, unreadable eyes.

*

'What are you doing here? Shouldn't you be at school?'
He is rubbing a yellow waxy substance into a gash on his palm.
'It's dinner hour,' she replies. 'I left something at home.'
The road feels unstable beneath her feet, like she might sink and fall. A long pause while he studies her. His mouth a crack in the roof of the world.
'He's gone you know. We took care of him.'
By his hand on the fence there hangs a row of freshly killed moles.

X V

The woman is running and her younger self is running and they are one.

*

They cross the lode, a narrow sike defining the bog's perimeter. On the lagg beyond is a sparse copse of birch, willow and alder. Through the trees is the raised plateau of the Moss itself. Forbidden territory. A sprawl of sudden mires, of unknown depths. A place of danger.

*

They run. Deftly navigating the hummocks of sphagnum and sedge that act as quivering stepping stones, each sinking under foot and oozing dark liquid.

*

But the countless channels, soaks and quicks stall their progress. They find a pole of birch and use it to test the depths of the water, but their progress slows to almost nothing. *If you ever need me*, he had said, *I'm often out here. I'm easy to find.* They scan the Moss, looking for him, for any sign of activity. Nothing. Utterly exhausted they sink to the ground and an impotent fury overwhelms them.

XVI

The woman is herself again. The great upswelling of memory has momentarily stilled. The day is darkening and she tracks her way slowly back across the Moss. She rests beneath a tree on the lagg as the stars begin to show. She looks up through its branches at the evening sky. The tree's trunk is split in two, like a tuning fork stuck into the earth. On the left-hand trunk there is a huge burr. A black eyeless face.

*

Colours. Darkening. Glimmer of stars reflecting in the water of the kolk at the centre of the Moss.

*

Later. Her childhood room. The remains of her narrow bed, dressing table and mirror. Stones arranged on the window sill. Dampness hanging in the air.

*

She watches darkness gather over the Moss. Fearful of sleep, and of what is to come.

*

There are things buried here. Things whose oldness you can only guess at. Do you dream? There is someone, a man, and he is at the centre. He is the pivot, about which all else moves. He is here, buried. Do you dream?

*

But when she falls into that dream she is no longer the victim. She is one of the throng. A mass of people who form a circle around him. Singing. A chant, filling the night air like static.

*

And he is looking at her. And there are words in his mouth, but she cannot make them out. A sister tongue, something long forgotten, unknowable. But the look in his eyes is a language beyond language, which speaks to the blood, to the heart. *Fear.*

*

And she watches as they wrap the cord around his neck, sink the knife into his side, and submerge him.

*

Water, drowning.

XVII

She is woken by a great ache in her belly. She has felt it
before, intermittently, but today it seems to intensify as
the morning unfolds.

*

A distant sound spills across the fields. A low, contin-
uous, watery note, minutes long, barely perceptible.
Calling to her blood. Singing the scars of her body, and
of her skinless skin.

*

Her looking out across the fields. Mist beginning to gather here and there, close to the ground. To the south, she knows, beyond sight, a campfire. Always burning. She thinks of him. His eyes, his frightened animal body. *The Moss. That's where you're headed?* She retrieves the small metallic figure from her pocket. As day reaches its full, meagre brightness she sets out.

*

To walk, and to carry my heart in my hands, heavy, glistening.

*

See her. Her face, her eyes. Fingers clenched. Something familial held between you. There.

*

She crosses the lode, over the lagg and onto the raised plateau. Rush of language leaving her.

*

Scene. A region of mire barely distinguishable from any other. But the surface of the bog falling away to reveal a shallow bank of peat. At the base of the bank is a fissure, scarcely three feet wide. It is brimming with bog water.

*

Colours. Blacks and browns. A creeping stain. The world turned the complexion of leather.

*

Beached on the far side of the narrow pool is a dark, tangled form. Once in the shape of a man, but compressed and contorted by the crushing embrace of peat and water. Century over century. A vessel fallen from the stars.

*

She is holding her breath. The pain in her belly sharpening to an excruciating point.

*

She knows nothing of Grauballe, of Tollund, of Cashel, but she knows him. Has known him from her youngest days. The dream of the Moss itself. Its murmuring song.

*

He is the pivot, about which all else moves. He is here, buried. Do you dream?

*

But some occult movement of the bog has exhumed him, thrusting him into the scouring daylight. His skin splitting, rupturing like bark.

*

'Don't worry,' her rescuer had said, all those years ago, as she sat drying before the campfire. 'I dream too.' And a spark of sympathy, of intimacy, had leapt between them.

*

And she had sensed it, dimly. His courage, his quiet
suffering.

'Here, take this, it will be our secret. It was my
grandmother's.'

'No. I couldn't.'

'You need it more than me, I think. Take it. And when
you have those dreams, you'll know you're not alone.'

*

She lifts the pendant from around her neck. A figurine
made of bog oak, black as charcoal.

*

The world tilts, spinning. This, its motionless centre.

*

Periapt. Effigy. Small fetish of death. Passed through countless generations, and now returned at last to its source.

*

She places it around his neck. His black, eyeless face stares back at her. She holds him. The weight of him. *This moment.*

*

Her parents. The bond of violence between them. The skin around her mother's eyes, swollen, discoloured. Her shoes wet and caked in mud, and the father gone, nowhere to be seen.

*

And the man who had saved her. His face, visible at last. His gentle voice. His reckless kindness.

*

And the nameless woman she had stowed in the shallow earth. Patron saint of suicides. A bloody cipher.

*

And the countless others, their lives and deaths, filling the air around her. A clamouring chorus.

*

But most of all him. His manifold deaths and the fear in his eyes.

*

His life and afterlife. A bright point amid darkness. Drawing everything to him. Gouge, shatter, scar, fracture. Moths to the flame.

XVIII

She releases him back gently into the water, where he slowly sinks into the silt of forgetting. The passing of hours. Her watching the pool's surface become placid again. Great seeming stillness of the world.

*

Deadened beauty of time. Slow vastness. Tender scour of ice and water. Life itself, rubbing, wearing, thinning. Becoming translucent.

*

The pain in her belly gradually, imperceptibly, ebbing away into nothing. Far off, in the woods to the south, a deep, guttural sound rings out. Echoing, reverberating.

*

ıces her steps back across the Moss, over the lagg, and through the fields beyond.

*

The mist is thicker now. Rubbing at the shapes of things. Gathering about her.

*

That sound again. Nearer. Almost tangible. Antlers. Tines. Eyes. Fear fading. The dying of stars.

*

She walks slowly towards it. Her form contracting, dissipating, diminishing, until she is a mere bruise on grey-white skin. And then gone.

Lightning Source UK Ltd.
Milton Keynes UK
UKHW021121260620
365563UK00011B/723

9 781916 393516